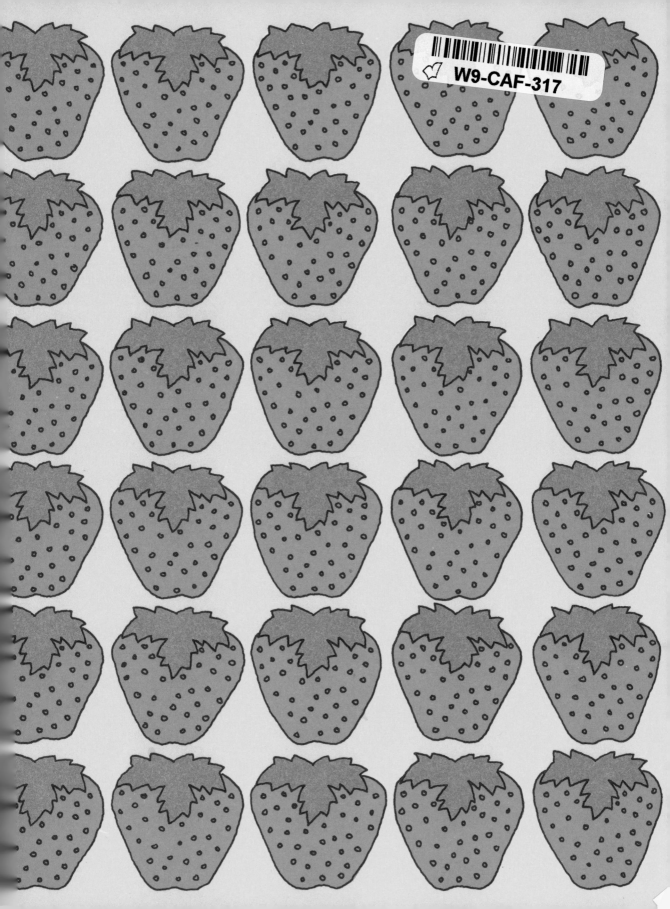

THE STICKYBEAR FAMILY ™

Bedford Stickybear   **Sara Stickybear**

Bumper Stickybear

this
strawberry library
of first learning
book
belongs to

Weekly Reader Books' Edition

Library of Congress Cataloging in Publication Data

Hefter, Richard.
    Where is the bear?

    (Stickybear books)
    Summary: Following a good breakfast, the Stickybear
family plays hide-and-go-seek.
    [1. Bears—Fiction. 2. Stories in rhyme] I. Title.
II. Series: Hefter, Richard. Stickybear books.
PZ8.3.H397Wh   1983   [E]   83-6296
ISBN 0-911787-06-2

where is the bear?

by Richard Hefter

Optimum Resource, Inc. • Connecticut

His shirt and his tie
Are right over there.
So are his shoes;
But where is the bear?

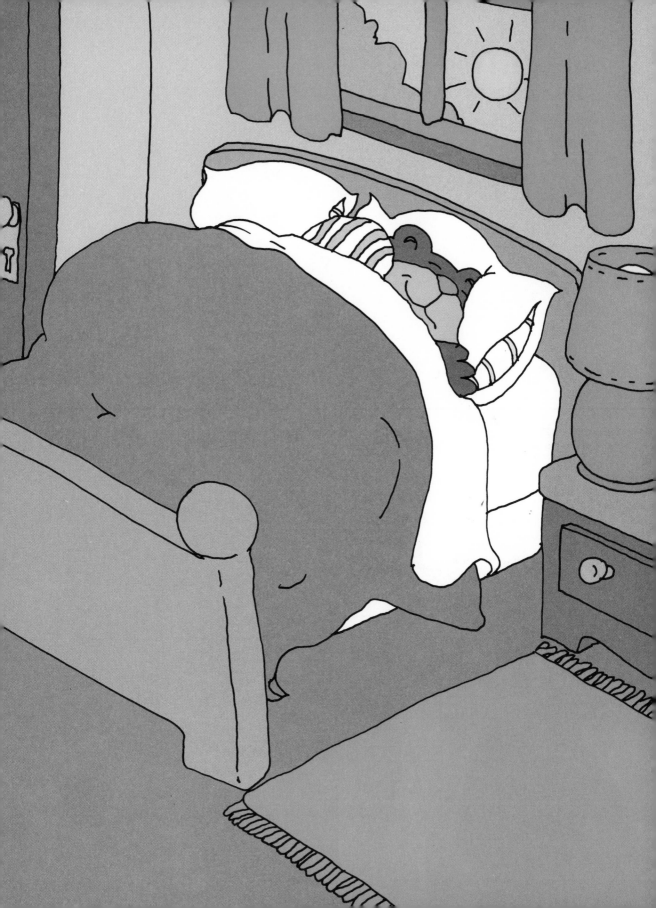

Breakfast is ready,
The table is set;
Sleepy old Stickybear
Isn't up yet.

Tizzy and Bumper
The littlest bears;
Are ready to eat
And coming downstairs.

The good morning smell
Of honey and bread;
Will get Stickybear up
And out of his bed.

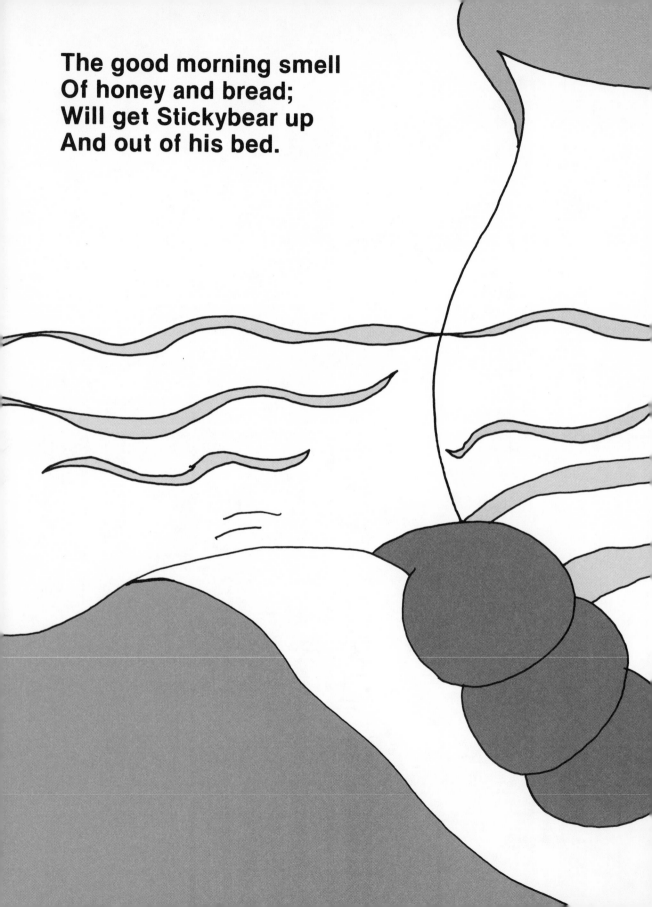

Cold milk and honey,
Sticky and sweet,
Pancakes and porridge;
A bear's favorite treat.

Still in his room
At the top of the stair;
Stickybear is putting on
His underwear.

Now in the bathroom,
Combing his hair,
And brushing his teeth
Is a clean, hungry bear.

Fresh fruit and eggs,
Juice, cold and sweet,
Cream and more honey;
Bears love to eat.

Stickybear is down now
Eating his food.
He is a bit late
But he's in a good mood.

Bumper and Tizzy
Have gone out to play;
Hide-and-go-seek
On a warm, sunny day.

**Bumper is hiding
Somewhere out there.
Look in the trees.
Can you find the bear?**

Now it is Tizzy's turn;
She's gone to hide.
Bumper can't find her.
Psst . . . look inside.

Now both little bears
Are hiding from you.
I know where they are.
Can you find them too?

The bears are both out now,
And they have a hunch,
That it's nearly time;
To munch a nice lunch.

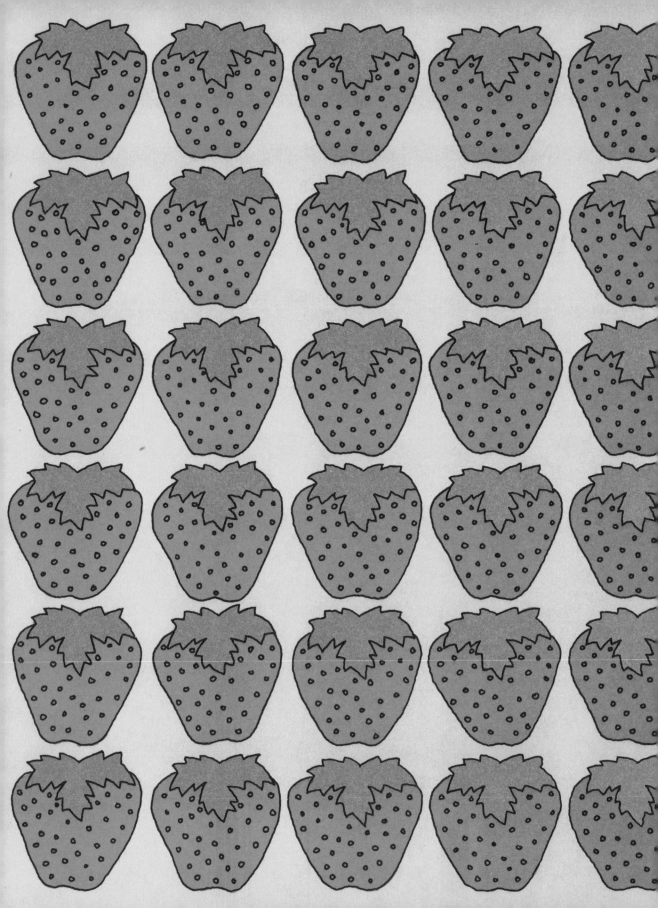